GHOST NINJA

Story and art by Blue Ocean

Ⓛ Ⓑ
Little, Brown and Company
New York · Boston

LEGO, the LEGO logo, the Brick and Knob configurations, the Minifigure,
NINJAGO and the NINJAGO logo are trademarks of the LEGO Group.

Produced by Little, Brown and Company under license
from the LEGO Group. © 2016 The LEGO Group.

Comic artwork © 2016 by Blue Ocean Entertainment AG, Germany

Stories written by Christian Hector
Pencils by Jon Fernandez
Inks by Ivan Solans
Colors by Oriol San Julian & Javi Chaler

Little, Brown and Company

Hachette Book Group
1290 Avenue of the Americas, New York, NY 10104
Visit us at lb-kids.com

Little, Brown and Company is a division of Hachette Book Group, Inc.
The Little, Brown name and logo are trademarks
of Hachette Book Group, Inc.

The publisher is not responsible for websites (or their
content) that are not owned by the publisher.

First Edition: March 2016

Library of Congress Control Number: 2015960163

ISBN 978-0-316-30922-6 (paper over board) — ISBN 978-0-316-26611-6 (pb)

10 9 8 7 6 5 4 3 2 1

LAKE

Printed in the United States of America

LLOYD

Mourning the loss of his father, Lloyd fears change and how it might affect his future. His fragile state will allow the cursed spirit of Morro to possess his body and transform him into the most dangerous threat the ninja will have ever faced.

KAI

After promising Lloyd his protection, Kai feels personally obligated to single-handedly save him. But in order to get his friend back, he'll have to trust the team. In the end, Kai will learn that they all have weaknesses, but it's one another's strengths that will lift them up.

COLE

Cole may seem like a big fraidycat at times, but he always comes through for his friends. He starts this season off scared of ghosts, but when he gets trapped in a haunted house at sunrise, he's permanently changed into one. At first, everything seems bleak, but soon Cole will learn that with a new outlook come new opportunities and new abilities.

JAY

As an avid fan of fantasy, Jay is in hog heaven to be on a quest filled with magical relics, mysterious riddles, and dangerous temple traps...but most of all he's excited to master "Cyclondo," a lost martial art that enables one to temporarily take flight.

MASTER WU + MISAKO

With an eye toward retirement, Master Wu and Misako have purchased a tea farm with the hope of starting a business. But when things get rough, they'll need everything, including the kitchen sink, to survive to see retirement.

GHOST NINJA

It is a Season of Change...

Since defeating Master Chen and his
army in the Tournament of Elements,
the ninja have never been more
united. Yet Lloyd mourns the loss of his
father to the Cursed Realm and questions
his path ahead. Kai makes a solemn
promise to look after Lloyd, as Nya looked
after Kai upon their parents' demise. But
that promise is put into jeopardy when a
cold wind blows through Ninjago...

The cursed spirit of Morro—the Master
of Wind, who also happens to be Master
Wu's first pupil—possesses Lloyd. Now,
without the aid of their elemental powers,
the remaining ninja must square off
against their brother, the Green Ninja.
The good and the bad race to find the Lost
Tomb of the First Spinjitzu Master, which
holds a powerful relic called the Realm
Crystal, which can not only affect Ninjago,
but also other hidden realms the ninja
have yet to discover...

THE NASTIEST OF THE NASTY!

THE KRYPTARIUM PRISON IS ALMOST EMPTY. COLE AND NINJAGO NEED EVERY MAN IN THE FIGHT AGAINST THE ACONDRAI. WELL, ALMOST EVERY MAN.

HA-HA. I'VE GOT A FUNNY FEELING...

AS THEY SIMPLY COULD NOT BE TRUSTED, THE NASTIEST OF THE NASTY VILLAINS ARE LEFT BEHIND: GENERAL KOZU, CAPTAIN SOTO, NO-EYED PETE, FRAKJAW, BONE-ZAI, AND THE TWO NINDROIDS.

BUT DUE TO THE RECENT TURMOIL, THE GUARDS HAVE BECOME CARELESS.

JUST A LITTLE FARTHER...

THIS WILL GET US OUT OF HERE!

CLICK!

THE ONLY ONES WHO CAN STOP THE DANGEROUS PARTY NOW ARE THE BUILDERS. OR CAN THEY?

UH, GUYS...I THINK WE'RE IN TROUBLE.

ER, WE DON'T MEAN ANY HARM. WE'RE JUST THE BUILDERS.

YOU COULDN'T HARM US ANYWAY, EVEN IF YOU WANTED TO!

A LITTLE LATER...

ALL CALM IN THE CITY BY THE LOOKS OF IT.

I'M STARVING. LET'S EAT SOMETHING.

I KNOW A GREAT PLACE ABOUT TEN FEET IN FRONT OF US...

I GIVE YOU ONE MINUTE TO BRING ME MY FOOD. IF IT COMES ANY LATER, WE'LL SMASH UP THIS PLACE!

WHAT ARE YA WAITING FOR? I'M HUNGRY!

KLONK

LOOKS LIKE SOMEONE SHOULD TEACH THOSE GUYS SOME MANNERS!

NOBODY WILL SMASH UP ANYTHING HERE! AND YOU'RE GOING TO APOLOGIZE TO THE WAITER RIGHT NOW!

WAITAMINUTE... I KNOW YOU!

SOTO!

BACK OFF, CHEEKY NINJA!

SWISH

16

SEVERAL DAYS LATER, THE NINJA ARE ON THEIR WAY BACK FROM A MISSION.

I WONDER IF WE'RE EVER GOING TO BE MASTERS OF AIRJITZU.

HEY, IS THAT LLOYD?! LET'S FOLLOW HIM THROUGH THAT GATE.

SWOOSH!

THE NINJA RUN THROUGH THE PORTAL AND...

WHY HAS HE STOPPED?

CAREFUL, GUYS!

JUST LOOK AT THOSE TREES!

WHERE ARE WE NOW?

AND MORE IMPORTANT: WHERE IS LLOYD?

AIRJITZU

SWOOSH!

WE DID IT!

THUMP

I FEEL MUCH MORE AWAKE ALREADY!

IS NYA OKAY?!

THUMP

NYA, WHAT'S THE MATTER?

LOOK AT HER EYES! THEY'RE GREEN!

NYA!

YOU'RE IN MY WAY, GHOULTAR!

UNFORTUNATELY FOR YOU, NINJA, YOU WON'T BE GOING THE WAY YOU THINK. YOU'LL BE GOING SOMEWHERE ELSE!

QUICK! THEY ARE TRYING TO ESCAPE INTO THE CITY!

THE GHOSTS MANAGE TO HIDE FROM THE NINJA IN NINJAGO CITY.

HUH, WHERE ARE THEY?

MY SCANNERS CAN'T LOCATE THEM ANYWHERE.

OH NO!

IN THE MIDST OF THE BATTLE, THE NINJA ARE SEPARATED.

THERE'S TOO MANY!

WE'RE SURROUNDED. BUT I HAVE AN IDEA!

IF WE BACK INTO THE CAGE, NO ONE CAN ATTACK US FROM BEHIND!

SMACK!

HUH. MAYBE THAT WASN'T SUCH A GREAT IDEA.

WHY?

THAT'S WHY!

AND SO BANSHA AND GHOULTAR'S PLAN WORKS AFTER ALL.

GREAT IDEA, KAI!

CREEEEAAAK

MIRROR, MIRROR

IN A SMALL VILLAGE ON THE OUTSKIRTS OF NINJAGO CITY, STRANGE THINGS ARE HAPPENING...

AAAAAAAH!

WHAT'S GOING ON?!

SO MUCH FOR A PLEASANT MEAL. HOW ARE ALL THESE THINGS FLYING ON THEIR OWN?!

HONEY, GO OUTSIDE WHERE IT'S SAFE. I'LL PUT AN END TO THIS INSANITY!

HONEY? ARE YOU OKAY? PLEASE SAY SOMETHING...

LET ME JUST PEEK IN THE WINDOW...

OH NO!

WHY WOULD THE GHOSTS CHASE THIS GOOD WOMAN HERE OF ALL PLACES?! THAT IS ODD.

COLE, JAY, GATHER THE OTHERS. GO FIND OUT WHAT'S HAPPENING. AND BE CAREFUL.

BUT WE HAVE TO RESCUE LLOYD.

SOMETIMES SOMETHING THAT APPEARS TO BE A STEP IN THE WRONG DIRECTION IS ACTUALLY A SHORTCUT.

JUST HALF AN HOUR LATER, ALL FOUR NINJA ARE HEADING TO THE VILLAGE TO INVESTIGATE.

WELL, IF YOU ASK ME, A STEP IN THE WRONG DIRECTION IS JUST A DETOUR.

MASTER WU HAS OFTEN BEEN RIGHT, KAI.

BESIDES, WE'LL BE HELPING DEFENSELESS VILLAGERS AGAINST HORRIBLE GHOSTS.

QUIET! I HAVE THE FEELING WE'RE BEING FOLLOWED.

GHOST TREES!

NOW I'M QUITE CERTAIN THAT WE'RE BEING FOLLOWED!

LET'S START PRUNING THEM!

NEVER MIND PRUNING THEM!

CUT THEM DOWN!

FUOOOOSH!

CRASH!

TOO BAD ABOUT THOSE TREES, BUT AT LEAST WE GOT RID OF THE SKREEMERS POSSESSING THEM.

MAYBE WE SHOULD KNOCK A HOLE IN THE MIRROR?!

NO, KAI! IF WE DESTROY THE MIRROR, THE TOWNSPEOPLE COULD BE TRAPPED FOREVER.

HAVE YOU GOT A BETTER IDEA?

KRACH

NO, I DON'T KNOW WHAT TO DO, EITHER.

I HAVE AN IDEA.

LUCKILY, GHOSTS CAN SIMPLY WALK INTO MIRRORS.

COOL! I FOUND ANOTHER ADVANTAGE TO BEING A GHOST!

COLE! LOOK OUT!

OH NO! THE POOR MAN IS ALSO POSSESSED.

THE LOST SCROLLS OF SPINJITZU

Welcome to the Ninjago World

The Ninjago world was created long ago by the First Spinjitzu Master using the power of the Golden Weapons.

Although this realm was initially a place of peace and light, evil arose in the person of the Overlord, who wished dominion over the planet. With no end to the struggle in sight, the First Spinjitzu Master took the drastic step of splitting the land of Ninjago in half. The

Overlord and his followers were trapped on a portion that came to be known as the Island of Darkness.

This was not the end of threats to the planet. The first Serpentine War pitted humans against snake warriors. One of the First Spinjitzu Master's sons, Garmadon, was corrupted by

darkness and tried to conquer the world, only to be defeated by his brother, Wu. Master Wu would go on to defend the planet against various menaces for years to come, before eventually recruiting a team of young ninja to help him.

Ninjago is a geographically diverse planet, with volcanoes, deserts, ice caps, dense forests and jungles, toxic bogs, and more. Only one city is known to exist, Ninjago City, but there are long-lost cities dotting the

landscape. There are also a large number of villages and farming communities.

The ninja's adventures have carried them all over the planet, and they have saved the Ninjago world many times over. Time will tell what excitement the future has in store for them!

Ninjago map

1. Golden Peaks
2. Master Chen's Island
3. Ninjago City
4. Anacondrai Tomb
5. Samurai X Cave
6. Steap Wisdom Tea Farm
7. Kryptarium Prison
8. Hiroshi's Labyrinth
9. Tomb of the First Spinjitzu Master
10. Tiger Widow Island
11. Temple of Airjitzu
12. Wailing Alps
13. Corridor of Elders
14. City of Stiix
15. Spirit Coves

RONIN! HERO OR VILLAIN?

The only master Ronin serves is the almighty dollar. He's a thief who's known to have made a few bad bets—including selling his soul to the Soul Archer. When his path intersects with the ninja, Ronin has a chance to make things right and be a hero for once. But what's in it for him?

MORRO, MASTER OF WIND

Morro was Master Wu's first pupil. Long ago, after seeing his command of the wind, Wu trained him to be the Green Ninja. But there was a darkness inside Morro and a thirst to be the best, like no other. This worried Wu, and when the

Golden Weapons didn't react in the Green Ninja ceremony, Wu tried to convince Morro to give up...but he wouldn't.

Wanting to prove Wu wrong, Morro went out in search of the Lost Tomb of the First Spinjitzu Master but never came back. Little did Wu realize, Morro was banished to the Cursed Realm, where he patiently waited to get a second chance to become the Green Ninja, and when Lord Garmadon opened the door while defeating Master Chen, Morro finally got his wish.

THE PREEMINENT

The Preeminent isn't just the ruler of the Cursed Realm, she IS the Cursed Realm. All encompassing, she has a primordial thirst to curse all that she touches. That means

she won't be satisfied with just Ninjago—she won't stop until she has devoured all sixteen realms.

SOUL ARCHER

Soul Archer never misses.
With his supernatural bow and
arrows, he always finds his target.
This Ghost Archer is Morro's
right-hand man and a menace to
the ninja. When he's not helping
Morro, he's out there collecting
souls and biding his time to leverage
them to aid his evil will when needed.

BANSHA

Bansha is a Ghost Sorceress
with the power to mind meld
and take over someone's body
from a distant location. She
also has a piercing
scream that can
shatter eardrums
and cause
catastrophic
havoc.

GHOULTAR

Dumb and strong, Ghoultar never second-guesses an order. As the ghost muscle of the group, Ghoultar can either be the strength needed to put the Ghost Generals over the top or the dead weight that will sink them.

WRAYTH

If you hear cackling and the rev of his ghost cycle, watch your back, because this Ghost Biker might be coming for you. Armed with a supernatural chain that can turn anyone into a ghost, Wrayth looks to tie the ninja up.

THE GHOST NINJA

The ninja have battled their share of baddies, but these ghosts prove to be one of their biggest challenges yet. Not only can they possess nearly anyone and anything around, but the only way to stop one is with either water or weapons made of Deepstone.

DEEPSTONE AEROBLADES

Deepstone is a rare mineral mined from the bottom of the ocean. Since it's the only solid that can make contact with an ethereal ghost, what better way to use it than with an Aeroblade—a boomerang-esque weapon that returns to its master...most of the time?

AIRJITZU

An ancient martial art created by Master Yang, Airjitzu allows a Spinjitzu Master to propel himself into the air and temporarily take flight. Or as Jay likes to call it—"Cyclondo!" It's a difficult art to master but integral to the ninja's mission.

THE REALM CRYSTAL

The Realm Crystal is so powerful, the First Spinjitzu Master kept it close to him at his hidden burial site because he didn't want it to fall into the wrong hands. The crystal has sixteen sides, and if exposed to light, it will open one of sixteen portals to other worlds. Morro is after the crystal because it is the only way for the Preeminent to cross over into Ninjago.

THE SWORD OF SANCTUARY

Though it looks like a normal sword, the Sword of Sanctuary foretells an opponent's next move within the reflection of its blade. Wielded properly, it's a devastating weapon that automatically gives the carrier the upper hand in battle, but it can also help guide its wielder through impossible traps and imminent danger.

THE ALLIED ARMOR OF AZURE

If ninja find themselves in a jam and in need of some help, they might want to wear this magical breastplate. If your opponent has it—look out, because at any moment he or she can conjure the aid of allies. When Morro steals it, he's able to usher a few ghost friends from the Cursed Realm.

STEEP WISDOM

Since Wu knows so much about teas, why not open a business? Much of the ninja's operations are run out of

Master Wu's tea farm—which is good, since they are struggling to find customers. When the ninja sell their shares to Ronin in exchange for some lifesaving help, Wu gets an unexpected business partner.

THE WAILING ALPS

The Wailing Alps are the tallest peaks in Ninjago and are named after the "wailing" wind gusts that could blow one clear off the mountain if not properly tied down.

They're cold, with unrelenting blizzards. As if these peaks weren't high enough, they are merely a stepping-stone to the Cloud Kingdom.

STIIX

If there's anything that smells worse than the coast, it's the dilapidated village of Stiix, which extends over it. In constant disrepair, Stiix is a rickety cesspool of fishmongers and vagrants...which is why it's the perfect home for Ronin and his pawnshop. Eventually, Stiix becomes Morro's headquarters and the location of the Preeminent's arrival.

THE CLOUD KINGDOM

There's a kingdom in the clouds, and the denizens of this regal realm are doing more than just looking down on Ninjago—they are writing its destiny! It was they who decided Lloyd should be the Green Ninja, that Zane should be a Nindroid, and that Cole would be a ghost. But just because they have written the past, doesn't mean they always know the future.

(After all, those who live in the Cloud Kingdom may know a person's destiny, but they don't always know how those who live below will arrive at it.)

THE LOST TOMB OF THE FIRST SPINJITZU MASTER

It is a place of legend, thought never to have existed. But after finding an encoded message on Master Wu's staff, the ninja discover it's real. To actually get there is another

thing entirely. First they'll need to learn Airjitzu so they can get to the Cloud Kingdom. Then they must procure the Sword of Sanctuary to see past the deadly puzzle traps protecting the jewel of the burial site—the all-powerful Realm Crystal.

THE LIBRARY IN DOMU

In this awe-inspiring place, you can find any book written on anything...ever!

Managed by monks and students of history, this location will prove a valuable source of knowledge and history. What secrets does Ninjago's mysterious past hold? You can find the answers here if you dig deep enough in the seemingly infinite collection of books.

YANG'S HAUNTED TEMPLE

There were other masters in Ninjago, and not all of them as sweet as Wu. Master Yang was hard on his students, but he is responsible for creating Airjitzu—just the coolest thing since Spinjitzu. The problem is, Master Yang is no longer around, and now his spirit haunts his temple, an architectural relic from a bygone era of Ninjago.

CAN YOU DECODE THE SECRET MESSAGE?

An image-only decoding puzzle page.